Simone
Even More
Monstrous!

To Babette, Adele, Charlie, and Billy

The comics on pages 20, 24, 43, and 45 were orginally published in *Simone, joli monstre!* in 2016 by Bayard Canada Livres.

Owlkids Books acknowledges the financial support of the Canada Council for the Arts, the Ontario Arts Council, the Government of Canada through the Canada Book Fund (CBF) and the Government of Ontario through the Ontario Media Development Corporation's Book Initiative for our publishing activities.

Published in Canada by
Owlkids Books Inc.
10 Lower Spadina Avenue
Toronto, ON M5V 2Z2

Published in the United States by
Owlkids Books Inc.
1700 Fourth Street
Berkeley, CA 94710

Library and Archives Canada Cataloguing in Publication

Simard, Rémy, author, illustrator
Simone, even more monstrous! / by Rémy Simard.

(Simone) ISBN 978-1-77147-300-2 (hardcover)

1. Graphic novels. I. Title.

PN6734.S55S54 2018 j741.5'971 C2017-904415-X

Library of Congress Control Number: 2017945883

Edited by: Karen Li
Designed by: Jaleesa Scotland

Manufactured in Dongguan, China, in November 2017, by Toppan Leefung Packaging & Printing (Dongguan) Co., Ltd.
Job #BAYDC51

A B C D E F

Publisher of Chirp, chickaDEE and OWL
www.owlkidsbooks.com

Owlkids Books is a division of

Simone

Even More Monstrous!

Written and illustrated by
Rémy Simard

Owlkids Books

The Blue-Eyed Nightmare

BOOM! BOOM!
WHO'S THERE?
YOU HAVE TO GUESS... I HAVE TWO ARMS AND TWO LEGS.
I'M SUPER CUTE, WITH BLONDE HAIR AND BIG BLUE EYES...
WHO AM I?
MY WORST NIGHTMARE!

A Monstrous Cold

YOU HAVE A MONSTER IN YOUR CLOSET?
THE CREEPIEST!
IT CALLS ITSELF A GIRL. REALLY SCARY STUFF!
SIMONE, ARE YOU THERE?
YES...
BUT I'M NOT FEELING WELL.
SHE'S CUTE!

All Eyes on Her

WOW! THAT IS ONE UGLY MONSTER!
I'M NOT UGLY.
I KNOW WHAT WOULD IMPROVE YOUR LOOKS. A WIG!
A WIG? BECAUSE I NEED MORE HAIR?
NO, BECAUSE YOU NEED MORE EYES!

Not Exactly Natural

MORRIS, WHY ARE YOU STILL IN BED?
ARE YOU SICK?
NO. IT'S RAINING OUTSIDE. AND NO ONE LIKES RAIN.
THAT'S NOT TRUE. PLANTS LOVE THE RAIN!
SINCE WHEN?

In Bad Taste

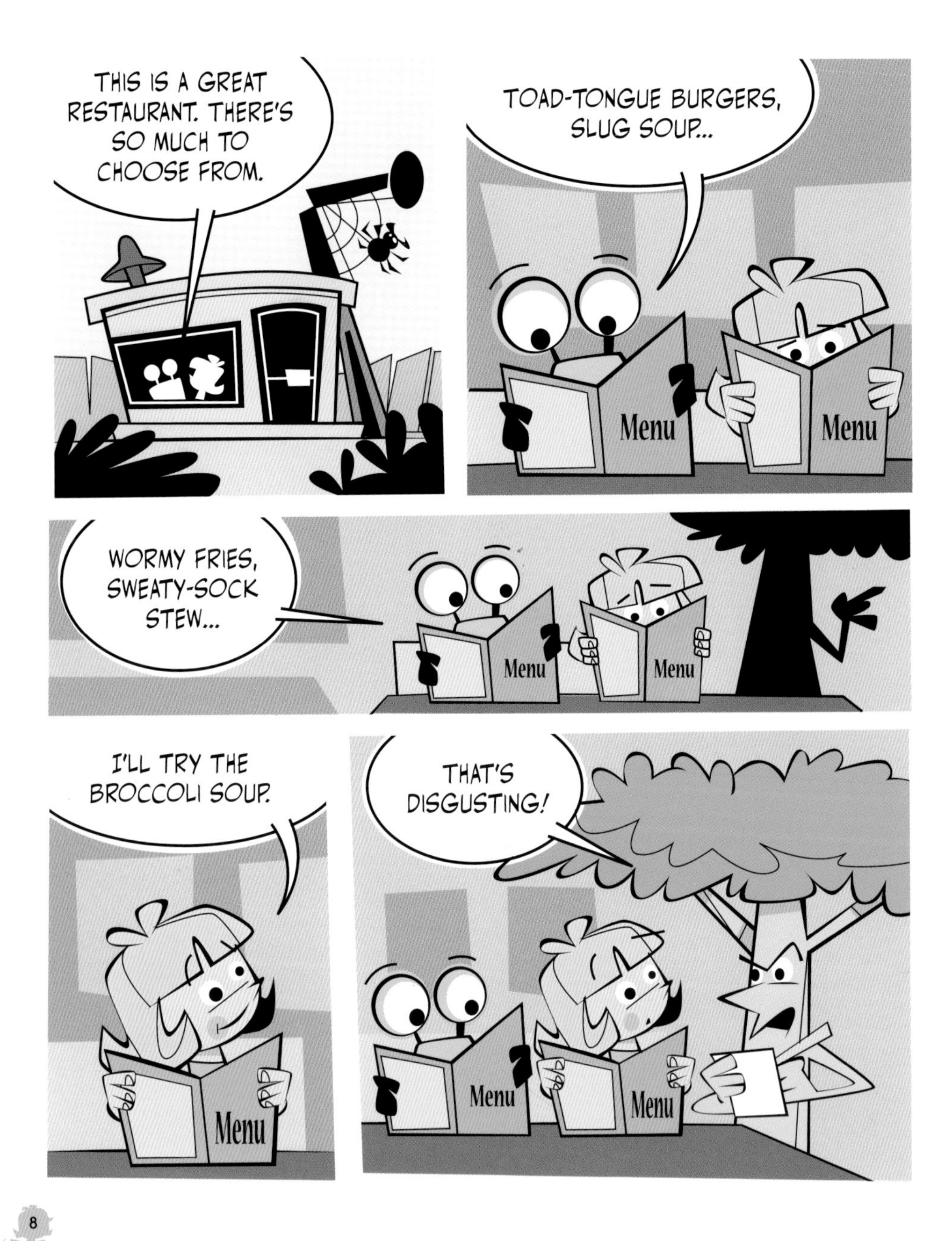
THIS IS A GREAT RESTAURANT. THERE'S SO MUCH TO CHOOSE FROM.
TOAD-TONGUE BURGERS, SLUG SOUP...
Menu
Menu
WORMY FRIES, SWEATY-SOCK STEW...
Menu
Menu
I'LL TRY THE BROCCOLI SOUP.
Menu
THAT'S DISGUSTING!
Menu
Menu

The Best Motivation

HI, SIMONE.
YOU'RE SWEATING. WHERE HAVE YOU BEEN?
I'VE BEEN TRAINING FOR A RACE.
A RACE? ARE YOU ANY GOOD?
WITH *MY* TRAINER...
I HAVE TO BE!
YUM! YUM!
HELP!

Don't Mess with Mums

OH, WHAT PRETTY FLOWERS.
THEY'LL MAKE A NICE BOUQUET.
I'D PUT THOSE BACK, IF I WERE YOU.
WHY?
THEIR MOM WON'T BE HAPPY.

A Priceless Friend

?
MORRIS, I DIDN'T KNOW YOU OWNED A PICASSO.
THAT'S NOT PICASSO.
THAT'S NORMAN!

Fur Real

PRR!
PRR!
PRR!
MORRIS, WHY IS YOUR CAT PURRING LIKE THAT?
HE LIKES YOU.
AND I THINK HE WOULD BE DISAPPOINTED IF...
PRR!
PRR!
...YOU DIDN'T PICK HIM UP.
PRR!

Block-a-Roni

MORRIS, HAVE YOU SEEN MY BUILDING BLOCKS?
NO.
WHAT ARE YOU COOKING?
PASTA! IN ALL DIFFERENT COLORS!
WANT A TASTE?

Beauty and the Beast

WHY DON'T YOU WANT TO PLAY HANSEL AND GRETEL?
IT'S NO FUN IF THE WITCH DOESN'T GET TO EAT THE KIDS.
WHAT IF WE PLAY BEAUTY AND THE BEAST?
YEAH! GREAT IDEA!
YOU'D MAKE AN AMAZING BEAST!

Digest and Seek

...98...99...100! READY OR NOT, HERE I COME!
THIS SHOULD BE EASY.
MORRIS PICKS THE WORST HIDING SPOTS.
THERE YOU ARE! FOUND YOU!
HOW ARE YOU SO GOOD AT THIS?

Just a Snack

SIMONE, QUICK! I NEED YOUR HELP!
I NEED 2 TONS OF STRAWBERRIES...
4 TONS OF BANANAS, 300 BUCKETS OF MILK, AND 1,000 CARTONS OF ICE CREAM.
ARE YOU MAKING MILKSHAKES FOR EVERYONE IN TOWN?
NO, JUST A FRIEND.
KONG

Garbage Day

QUICK, SIMONE! HELP ME!
WHAT'S GOING ON?
I THREW MY LITTLE BROTHER IN THE GARBAGE.
MOM'S REALLY MAD! SHE SAYS I HAVE TO FISH HIM OUT.
SO WHAT'S THE PROBLEM?
I NEED TO CATCH THE GARBAGE BAG!

Fashion Victim

LITTLE GIRL, YOU WILL LOOK SO PRETTY IN THIS DRESS!
YOU THINK?
IT WAS MADE JUST FOR YOU!
SHE'S MAGNIFICENT!

Keep Your Eyes on the Ball

WHAT'S WRONG, MORRIS?
WE'RE GOING TO LOSE THIS GAME.
BUT YOU'RE ON A GOOD TEAM.
WE'VE NEVER WON AGAINST THESE GUYS.
THEY'RE THAT GOOD?
IT'S NOT THAT.
THEY'RE INVISIBLE!

Slow Roast

HEY, SIMONE! MY PARENTS WANT TO INVITE YOU FOR SUPPER!
THAT'S NICE. WHEN DO WE EAT?
THE CHICKEN'S ALREADY ON THE BARBECUE...
IT SHOULD BE READY IN FOUR OR FIVE MONTHS!

Itchy Endings

THEY WERE MARRIED AND LIVED HAPPILY EVER AFTER.

THEY WERE MARRIED AND SUFFERED FROM TERRIBLE RASHES FOREVER.

WHAT A GREAT STORY!
THE MOST BEAUTIFUL ENDING I'VE EVER HEARD!

Burning Up

SIMONE! I HAVE A FRIEND WHO NEEDS YOUR HELP.
I THINK HE'S SICK.
DOES HE HAVE A FEVER?
WHAT'S THAT?
IT'S WHEN YOUR FOREHEAD FEELS HOT TO THE TOUCH.
OH, THEN HE'S SUPER SICK!
I TOLD YOU, I'M FINE!

No Strings Attached

GET LOST, YOU BIG BAD WOLF!
I DIDN'T KNOW THERE WERE PUPPET SHOWS IN YOUR WORLD.
"PUPPET"?
WHAT'S THAT?
SEE YOU TOMORROW, OMAR.

Half-Baked

WHY ARE WE GOING TO THE BEACH?
TO VISIT EDMOND!
HE'S BEEN SUNTANNING FOR 32 DAYS NOW.
WHAT?! DOESN'T HE KNOW HOW DANGEROUS THAT IS?
DON'T WORRY. HE DOES THIS EVERY YEAR.
HI, EDMOND! I BROUGHT YOU SOME MUSTARD!
GREAT!

Bath Time!

MORRIS, WHERE'S YOUR LITTLE BROTHER? I HOPE YOU DIDN'T TRY TO EAT HIM AGAIN.
NO, HE'S GETTING WASHED.
I LOOKED IN THE BATHROOM. HE'S NOT IN THE TUB.
I PUT HIM IN THE WASHING MACHINE. GENTLE CYCLE.

Caution: Stars Above

WHAT ARE YOU DOING, SIMONE?
I'M LOOKING AT THE STARS.
WELL, I WOULDN'T STAY THERE, IF I WERE YOU.
WHY NOT?

IN MY WORLD, STARS ARE LIKE BIRDS.

THEY POOP!
SPLAT!

Delivered Fresh to Your Door!

DING, DONG!
THAT'S PROBABLY THE PIZZA.
I'LL GET IT.
BING! BANG! NOM! NOM!
?
HERE'S YOUR PIZZA!
YOU'RE NOT EATING?
I'M NOT HUNGRY ANYMORE. THE DELIVERY GUY WAS DELICIOUS!

Out of Gas

WHY DO WE NEED A RIDE? YOUR SCHOOL ISN'T FAR.
I TOLD YOU, ROGER IS HAPPY TO DRIVE US.
SURE, BUT WHEN WILL WE GET GOING?
WHEN HE WAKES UP.
ZZZZZ...

Empty Net

HEY, SIMONE! THIS SPORT YOU TAUGHT US IS AWESOME.
HOCKEY!
WE'VE BEEN PLAYING FOR HOURS! AT FIRST IT WAS HARD TO SCORE.
BUT THEN NOTHING COULD STOP US.
OH, YEAH? WHY?
EASY.
WE ATE THE GOALIE!

Whiff of the Wild

SNIFF! SNIFF!
EWW! SOMETHING STINKS!
IT'S MOM'S NEW PERFUME: WILD SKUNK!
MORRIS! WHAT IS THAT HORRIBLE SMELL?

You Win Some, You Lose Some

MORRIS, YOU HAVE TO STOP EATING YOUR FRIENDS.
BUT THAT'S WHAT FRIENDS ARE FOR!
WELL, WHAT ABOUT ME?
YOU'RE NOT VERY APPETIZING.
WHY DON'T YOU TRY EATING OTHER THINGS? LIKE CUCUMBERS? OR MUSHROOMS?
GREAT IDEA!
HERE, LITTLE MUSHROOMS!

A Clean Conscience

MORRIS, TIME TO WASH UP.
BUT MOM, I WASHED LAST YEAR.
GET IN THE SHOWER.
I HATE GETTING WET.
I HAVE AN IDEA...
H
C

Closing Time

OOOH, A MUSEUM! LET'S GO INSIDE!
MUSEUM
HMM... I THINK WE'RE TOO LATE.
MUSEU
THE WORKERS ARE HEADING HOME.
MUSEUM OF
GOOD NIGHT, PICASSO!
SEE YOU TOMORROW.

Lunar Landing

SIMONE, LOOK HOW HIGH I CAN THROW THESE ROCKS!
YOU SHOULD BE CAREFUL.
YOU COULD HIT...
SMACK!
THUD!
...THE MOON.
OW.

Dangerous Delivery

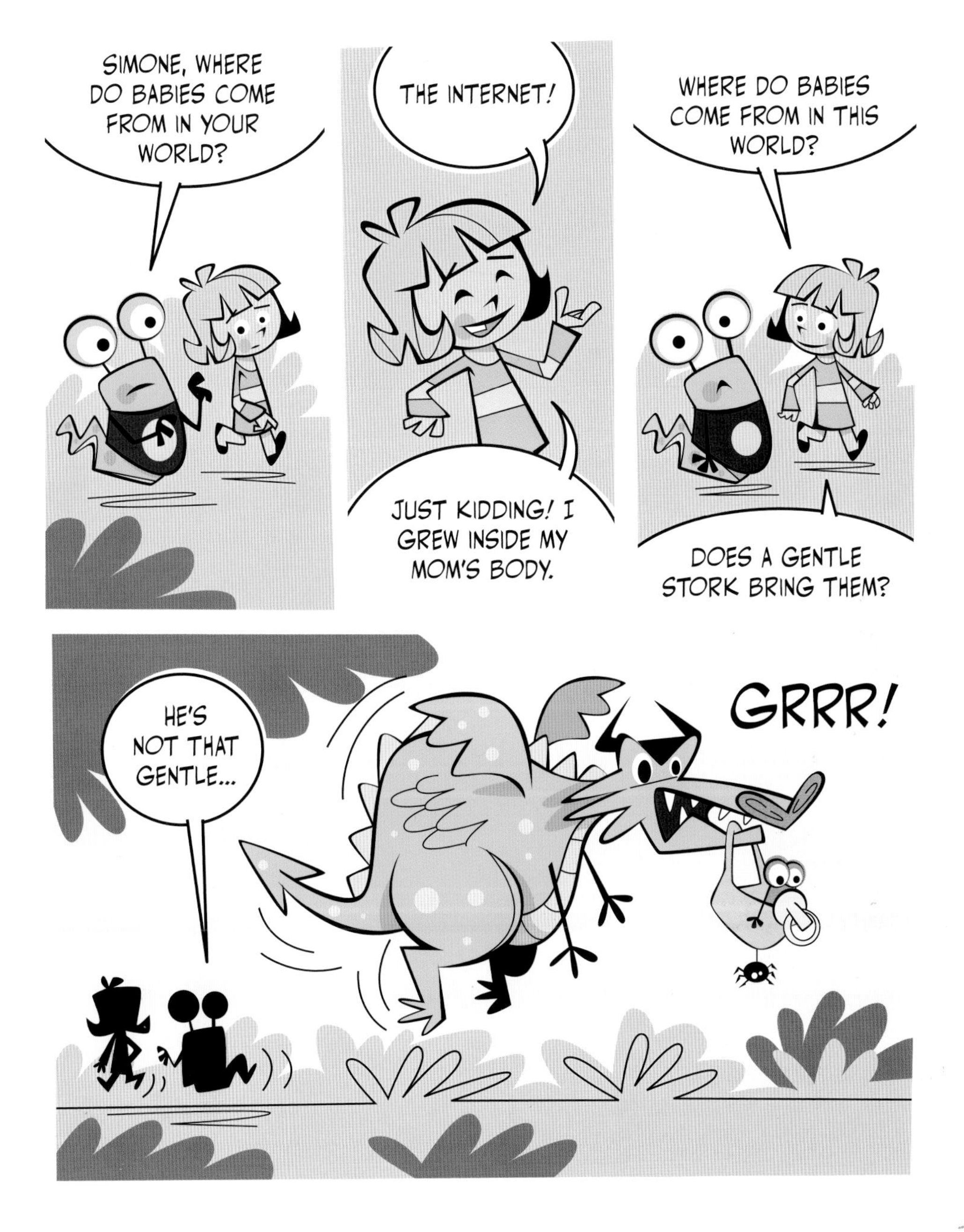
SIMONE, WHERE DO BABIES COME FROM IN YOUR WORLD?
THE INTERNET!
JUST KIDDING! I GREW INSIDE MY MOM'S BODY.
WHERE DO BABIES COME FROM IN THIS WORLD?
DOES A GENTLE STORK BRING THEM?
HE'S NOT THAT GENTLE...
GRRR!

Kong Quake!

BOOM!
BOOM!
WHAT'S HAPPENING?
I TOLD YOU IT WAS A BAD IDEA TO GIVE A JUMP ROPE...
...TO KING KONG!
KONG
BOOM! BOOM! BOOM!

The Monster Outside Your Closet

HELLO! YOU MUST BE SIMONE!
YOU ARE SCARY! YOU'LL BE PERFECT TO BABYSIT MY KIDS.
DO YOU NEED ME TO FEED THEM? GIVE THEM A BATH?
NOPE! DON'T LIFT A FINGER.
KIDS! YOU'D BETTER STAY IN THE CLOSET. THE MONSTER'S HERE!
AAAHHH!

A Tough Girl to Swallow

WHAT'S FOR LUNCH TODAY?
I FEEL LIKE EATING A BURGER.
WITH LOTS OF FRIES AND KETCHUP. YOU?
I'M NOT SURE.
I'LL HAVE TO FIND A RECIPE FOR THIS ONE.

A Big Request

HELLO! I'M SIMONE, YOUR NEW BABYSITTER.
YOU SEEM A BIT... SMALL.
DON'T WORRY. I HAVE MY BABYSITTING CERTIFICATE.
I'M GREAT AT PLAYING WITH KIDS AND GETTING THEM TO EAT.
DO YOU KNOW HOW TO CHANGE DIAPERS?

In Stitches

SIMONE, IT'S A DISASTER!
ANDY'S BEEN HIT BY A CAR!
WE HAVE TO CALL AN AMBULANCE! OR A DOCTOR!
A DOCTOR? WE DON'T NEED A DOCTOR.
WE NEED A GOOD TAILOR...
...TO STITCH HIM BACK TOGETHER AGAIN!

Baby Overload

YOU DON'T HAVE TO WORRY. I'M AN EXCELLENT BABYSITTER!
I'VE HEARD! BUT YOU ONLY HAVE TWO HANDS!
HOW WILL YOU GIVE THEM THEIR BOTTLES?
HOW MANY BABIES DO YOU HAVE?
275!

Sticky Snowfall

WOO-HOO! IT SNOWED! LET'S PLAY OUTSIDE!
?
YUCK! GROSS!
THAT'S NOT SNOW. IT'S SHAVING CREAM FOR THE LAWN.

What's in a Name?

HEY, LARDBALL— CATCH!
MORRIS, YOU SHOULD BE ASHAMED!
ASHAMED? WHY?
IT'S NOT NICE TO CALL NAMES. YOU COULD HURT HIS FEELINGS.
BUT... THAT *IS* HIS NAME!
FROSTY THE LARDBALL!

Old Family Recipe

15 SLUG EYES, 3 ROTTEN ONIONS, 1 OLD SOCK...
A HANDFUL OF RABBIT DROPPINGS, 4 CROW FEATHERS, TOAD SWEAT...
...AND A GALLON OF RED PAINT.
WHAT ARE YOU MAKING?
SPAGHETTI SAUCE!

Out of Step

COME ON, SIMONE. FOLLOW THE RHYTHM.
MADAME ESTELLE'S SCHOOL OF DANCE
JUST DO WHAT I DO.
1, 2...
3, 4...
5, 6...
7, 8.
CLEARLY, THE OCTOPUS DANCE IS NOT FOR YOU.

Royal Rags

SANTA!
SANTA!
SANTA!
SANTA!
THE LITTLE BLONDE GIRL WROTE YOU.
OH, NO. WHAT DOES SHE WANT NOW?
A PRINCESS DRESS!
THAT'S EASY!
CINDERELLA GAVE ME HERS.
IT'S BEAUTIFUL!

Beware of Snow

SIMONE, WAIT! YOU CAN'T GO OUTSIDE!
WHY? WHAT'S WRONG?
THERE'S A HEAVY SNOWFALL WARNING.
COOL!
LIKE, REALLY HEAVY.

Festive Veggie

SIMONE! I'VE BEEN WAITING FOR YOU!
TAKE A LOOK. I DID WHAT YOU SAID.
I TOOK YOUR CHRISTMAS DECORATIONS...
AND YOU DECORATED A CHRISTMAS TREE?
NOT A TREE.
A CHRISTMAS BROCCOLI!